Yoshi's Yard

The Sound of Y

by Joanne Meier and Cecilia Minden · illustrated by Bob Ostrom

The Child's World

Published by The Child's World®
1980 Lookout Drive
Mankato, MN 56003-1705
800-599-READ
www.childsworld.com

The Child's World®: Mary Berendes, Publishing Director
The Design Lab: Design and page production

Library of Congress Cataloging-in-Publication Data
Meier, Joanne D.
  Yoshi's yard : the sound of Y / by Joanne Meier and
Cecilia Minden ; illustrated by Bob Ostrom.
     p. cm.
  ISBN 978-1-60253-423-0 (library bound : alk. paper)
  1. English language—Consonants—Juvenile literature.
2. English language—Phonetics—Juvenile literature. 3.
Reading—Phonetic method—Juvenile literature. I. Minden,
Cecilia. II. Ostrom, Bob. III. Title.
  PE1159.M49 2010
  [E]—dc22   2010005612

Printed in the United States of America in Mankato, MN.
July 2010
F11538

NOTE TO PARENTS AND EDUCATORS:

The Child's World® has created this series with the goal of exposing children to engaging stories and illustrations that assist in phonics development. The books in the series will help children learn the relationships between the letters of written language and the individual sounds of spoken language. This contact helps children learn to use these relationships to read and write words.

The books in this series follow a similar format. An introductory page, to be read by an adult, introduces the child to the phonics feature, or sound, that will be highlighted in the book. Read this page to the child, stressing the phonic feature. Help the student learn how to form the sound with her mouth. The story and engaging illustrations follow the introduction. At the end of the story, word lists categorize the feature words into their phonic elements.

Each book in this series has been carefully written to meet specific readability requirements. Close attention has been paid to elements such as word count, sentence length, and vocabulary. Readability formulas measure the ease with which the text can be read and understood. Each book in this series has been analyzed using the Spache readability formula.

Reading research suggests that systematic phonics instruction can greatly improve students' word recognition, spelling, and comprehension skills. This series assists in the teaching of phonics by providing students with important opportunities to apply their knowledge of phonics as they read words, sentences, and text.

This is the letter y.

In this book, you will read words that have the **y** sound as in: *yard, yellow, yell,* and *yet.*

4

Yoshi is playing in his yard.

It is a big yard!

There are yellow flowers.

8

Boys like to play in Yoshi's yard. They can yell and run fast.

Yoshi's friend York comes to play. "What do you want to do today?" asks Yoshi.

"Let's play on your
yellow slide," says York.
"You go first."

Yoshi goes first. He yells the whole way down.

York goes next.

He yells even more.

"Yoshi," says his mother.

"Are you okay?

I heard yelling."

"Yes, we're fine," says Yoshi.

"We're not done yet!"

Fun Facts

Yellow is a *primary* color. Red and blue are also primary colors. A primary color cannot be made from other colors. You can create other colors by mixing primary colors. You can make orange by mixing yellow and red. You can create green by mixing yellow and blue.

During times of war, you might notice trees with yellow ribbons tied around them. These ribbons express hope that men and women who are serving in the war will return home safely.

You might think people yell only when they're angry, but this isn't always true. Before there were newspapers, town criers let everyone know what was going on in the world. These people read the news aloud throughout the town. They had to yell the information so people could hear what they had to say.

Activity

Creating Colors

Gather yellow, red, and blue paints. Put each color in its own bowl or cup. Mix a little yellow and a little red on a paper plate. See what color you get. Keep experimenting to see all the different shades of orange you can create using different amounts of yellow and red. Next try combining yellow and blue. Finally, paint a picture using all the different colors you have created.

To Learn More

Books
About the Sound of Y
Moncure, Jane Belk. *My "y" Sound Box®*. Mankato, MN: The Child's World, 2009.

About Yards
Herman, Gail, and Jerry Smath (illustrator). *Buried in the Backyard*. New York: Kane Press, 2003.
Rockwell, Anne F., and Harlow Rockwell. *My Back Yard*. New York: Macmillan Publishing Co., 1984.

About Yelling
Eschbacher, Roger, and Adrian Johnson (illustrator). *Nonsense! He Yelled*. New York: Dial Books for Young Readers, 2002.
Sondheimer, Ilse, and Dee deRosa (illustrator). *The Boy Who Could Make His Mother Stop Yelling*. Fayetteville, NY: Rainbow Press, 1982.

About Yellow
Hillert, Margaret, and Ed Young (illustrator). *The Yellow Boat*. Chicago, IL: Norwood House Press, 2009.
Stewart, Melissa. *Why Are Animals Yellow?* Berkeley Heights, NJ: Enslow Publishers, 2009.

Web Sites
Visit our home page for lots of links about the Sound of Y:

childsworld.com/links

Note to Parents, Teachers, and Librarians: We routinely check our Web links to make sure they're safe, active sites—so encourage your readers to check them out!

Y Feature Words

Proper Names
York
Yoshi

Feature Words in Initial Position
yard
yell
yelling
yellow
yes
yet
you
your

About the Authors

Joanne Meier, PhD, has worked as an elementary school teacher, university professor, and researcher. She earned her BA in early childhood education from the University of South Carolina, and her MEd and PhD in education from the University of Virginia. She currently works as a literacy consultant for schools and private organizations. Joanne lives in Virginia with her husband Eric, daughters Kella and Erin, two cats, and a gerbil.

Cecilia Minden, PhD, is the former director of the Language and Literacy Program at the Harvard Graduate School of Education. She is now a reading consultant for school and library publications. She earned her PhD in reading education from the University of Virginia. Cecilia and her husband, Dave Cupp, live outside Chapel Hill, North Carolina. They enjoy sharing their love of reading with their grandchildren, Chelsea and Qadir.

About the Illustrator

Bob Ostrom has been illustrating children's books for nearly twenty years. A graduate of the New England School of Art & Design at Suffolk University, Bob has worked for such companies as Disney, Nickelodeon, and Cartoon Network. He lives in North Carolina with his wife Melissa and three children, Will, Charlie, and Mae.